S0-ACB-148

Concord
South Side

Betty Doll

satin shoes

Betty Doll

Patricia Polacco

PUFFIN BOOKS

for my dearest little friend,
Aunt Mala
Chicago. It
wonderful
ever forget
know
make
better.
It all started

From Patricia

When my mother passed away, I packed up her home and belongings and shipped the boxes to Michigan, where I now make my home. I did not open those cartons until almost a year after her death. As I finally went through her beloved things, holding them, remembering, smelling her scent still with them, I found a small box wrapped in brown paper with her handwriting on the outside: for my dearest little trisha.

When I opened the box, I reached in and pulled out a small handmade doll. I instantly remembered her as being the doll that my mother made when she was but six years old. Each little stitch was still in place and formed Betty Doll. Wrapped around her was a handwritten letter tied with a blue satin ribbon. When I opened the letter, I realized that Mom knew I would be reading it after her death.

In this story I would like to share her words with you, for in the face of bitter grief, her sweet words brought comfort, insight and warmth that still linger in my heart . . . and will continue to, as long as there are children who tell children about mothers they love.

My Darlin' Trisha, my mother wrote, I don't feel that great today, so I won't be going to the opera with Ginny tonight. I thought, instead, that I'd write this to you because I know that someday you'll read this when your heart is aching.

I guess Betty Doll was born, or made, right after our farmhouse burned to the ground on an especially cold fall night.

We all went to stay with Uncle Scott and Aunt Lois on Dunks Road until Dad and our neighbors could help to rebuild the smaller tar-paper house that escaped the flames on our farmstead.

All five of my dollies perished in that fire. I was so sad. Momma saw how much I missed them.

One day, Momma found some material in Aunt Lois's cloth box.

"Mary Ellen . . . today we are going to make you a new little dolly!" Momma said. She helped me cut her out. I sewed the seams together all by myself, stitch by stitch. Then Momma found some old pillow stuffing and I filled her up. When I sewed her, I felt that she was so perfect.

"What are you going to do about her face, Mary Ellen?" Momma asked.

I knew exactly what she looked like in my heart. So when I started to embroider her face, it just came . . . simple as that . . . it came! She had beautiful sky blue eyes, a delicate nose and a sweet pink mouth, almost like a little bow. Then I named her Betty!

Betty was with me wherever I went that year. She watched as Dad and my uncles and neighbors helped build our new house out of that old tar-paper shack. When it was finished, it was a sweet fieldstone cottage. After we moved in, Betty sat on the shelf across from my bed in my new bedroom. She'd come and get in bed with me when there were fierce Michigan thunderstorms.

She and I attended our first big party to celebrate our new home. She danced with me. When she was tired, we stood and watched Momma and Dad's friends twirl around the yard.

I even took Betty Doll with me on my first day at Smith School on Girard Road on the corner just one road away from our house. I felt excited, but scared, too. I could tell that Betty felt the same.

Betty and I had very formal tea parties. High tea! We'd get all dressed up like famous actors and do plays for each other. I liked to be Theda Bara. Betty liked to be Edna Purviance. Sometimes I was Sarah Bernhardt and she was Rudolph Valentino. Betty watched me say dramatic lines, and then I'd watch Betty recite poems.

In December, the school board closed our little country school. Then my brothers and I had to go all the way to Union City to school, almost five miles away. Betty was good company on the long walks to and from school.

"Mary Ellen, you're getting too old to carry that doll around with you!" my brother Richard said to me.

"I am not!" I said. But Richard and my brother George teased me about having her in my book bag.

One December day, it suddenly started to snow. It was light at first, but then it came down more and more.

The wind came up. It bit our faces and chapped our lips.

I started to get scared because we had almost two miles to go before we would be home, and the snow seemed to get heavier and heavier. After a while the snowfall turned into a blizzard. Snowdrifts were burying the road in front of us.

My brother George remembered the rickety old bridge over Mudsock Creek. "We'll be out of the blizzard if we rest under that bridge," he said as he pushed Richard and me down the bank and under the bridge. "We'll just stay here until someone comes to look for us."

We huddled together—the cold was raw and mean and made our faces sting. When I reached for Betty Doll, she wasn't there. She must have fallen out of my book bag. I started to cry. I just knew that Betty Doll was buried in mountains of snow.

My tears started freezing on my face. That's when George decided to make for home.

"Both of you stay here, I'm gonna bring back some help, I promise!"

Richard and I hugged and tried to blow warm breath into each other's hands. We were there for a very long time. We could hardly keep our eyes open, but we both remembered our father telling us never, ever to fall asleep if we were trapped out in the cold during a storm.

Once we heard a car slowly driving over the bridge, but we were both too weak to get up and scream for help. We prayed that George would find Dad and they would rescue us. As I was falling into a numb sleep, all I could think of was Betty Doll. I hoped that she wouldn't feel the terrible cold. I hoped that she was not lonely.

I don't know how much time passed, but it seemed like a dream when Richard and I felt our father's arms around us.

"Here are my lost little lambs," he whispered as he hugged and kissed us both. Then he opened a thermos full of hot sugared tea.

"And look who I found!" George said. He handed me Betty Doll.

"Where was she?" I sputtered.

"Right next to the road, near the bridge. The snowplow must have turned her up. Lucky it did, too, because if we hadn't seen her, we wouldn't have known where to find you two. The snow is so deep that we couldn't even see the bridge or creek."

Dad and George brought the cutter. He had heated soapstones on the floorboards. He covered Richard and me with a thick, warm blanket. I held Betty Doll so close. She had saved our lives. Richard and George never said anything about her again.

After the blizzard I got very sick. Perhaps it was the cold of that day, but I came down with some sort of fever that eventually damaged my heart. I wasn't allowed to run and play like other children for one whole summer! I loved climbing trees and swimming, but that was out of the question.

Betty didn't seem to care that we couldn't run and jump. She still smiled at me and we read lots of books together. Then we'd have such interesting conversations.

When I got well, Momma and Dad felt that since I had spent such a dismal summer I could go on a train trip all the way to Chicago to visit my aunt Mala and uncle Hugh.

Betty sat with me on the train. We were both so excited! Aunt Mala and Uncle Hugh met me at the train station. Then we rode in a real cab to their apartment on Water Street. Aunt Mala was so glamorous. She always looked like a movie actress.

We did wonderful things there in Chicago. We went to art museums,

the zoo . . . and such fancy restaurants. I noticed that Betty's dress was no longer suitable for such elegant surroundings. Especially since the blizzard. She needed a new one.

Aunt Mala had done such wonderful things for me already, I didn't want to ask her for some cloth to make Betty a new dress. But in the dresser in my room I found a blue dress folded in the bottom of the drawer. I knew that Aunt Mala had no more use for it, or it wouldn't be in the bottom drawer. So I cut a portion of the very full skirt out to make a dress for Betty.

Betty watched me sew. I could see her smile at the thought of that beautiful dress. Finally it was done. She looked so beautiful in it!

But when Aunt Mala saw the new dress, she gasped. "Mary Ellen, where did you get this material?"

"Out of the drawer, in the bottom of the bureau," I answered.

"Oh, my girl . . . my dear girl. That was my finest crepe de chine dress!"

At first she was very angry. "Why didn't you ask me before you cut it up?" she cried. But after a time, when she saw that I was undone, she calmed down. "Oh, Mary Ellen . . . it's all right, dear. It's all right. Don't cry," she said as she tried to comfort me. "Let's see what can be done."

Then we scurried into her sewing room with what was left of her dress.

We sewed all afternoon. The skirt had been so full that there was even enough to make me a dress, too. Then Aunt Mala asked Uncle Hugh to wait in the parlor while the three of us—my aunt, Betty Doll, and I—got dressed for dinner.

"I think this is much more stylish than before, don't you, Hugh?" she sang out as she twirled into the room. The dress was short now . . . but so much more beautiful. Then Betty and I made our entrance. We all looked so elegant. From that time on, whenever I looked at Betty Doll, I remembered that wonderful summer with Aunt Mala and Uncle Hugh.

As the years passed, Betty was witness to many family celebrations and momentous occasions. Some big and grand and some so small that no one but Betty knew of them.

She was there for the great flood in Union City in '29. She comforted me when my best friend got polio—folks said she probably got it from the swimming hole we all swam in. She watched from her place on my dressing table as I grew taller and my body changed from a little girl into a young woman. She waved good-bye when my brothers left home and went away to college, and cried with me the day my brother Richard went away to war.

I put her in my suitcase when I, too, left home and went away to college. She sat on my dresser in the dorm, and then in Mrs. Borchst's boarding house when I got my first teaching job.

More time passed. I married your father, and eventually gave birth to your brother and then you, my dear. Betty watched both of you as you played and cooed. She knew that you two were the best things that ever happened to me.

Then we all came back to Gramma's and Gramp's in Union City when I got a divorce. Betty took her place again on my dresser in my old room. That was the summer that Gramma got very sick.

I moved Betty into Gramma's room. On lazy summer afternoons, Gramma and I would sit and talk about the day she helped me sew Betty. It helped us to remember all of the things that we had done together and the milestones of our family on that little farm. You held Betty and listened to our stories.

After Gramma died, we sold the farm and prepared for our move to California.

"Where did Gramma go?" I remember you asking.

"She went on a long journey ahead of us," I answered.

"Why can't we go with her?" you asked.

"We have to stay and wait . . . wait for your children to be born someday."

You held Betty Doll all the way to California. I knew that she'd make you feel better.

In our house in Oakland, Betty Doll took her place on the bookshelf in my bedroom. The only times that she was removed and loaned out were when you needed her. Do you remember that?

Such a parade she watched from that shelf. You and your brother growing up. Your graduations, your engagements, your marriages.

The arrival of all ten of my grandchildren. So many wonderful little souls. Your brother Richard's eight, and your two.

Betty Doll came off that shelf for each and every one of them. She kissed away tears, soothed hurt knees and was a guest at hundreds of tea parties and slumber nights.

When all of the grandchildren grew too old to play with her, Betty went back in a place of honor on that shelf.

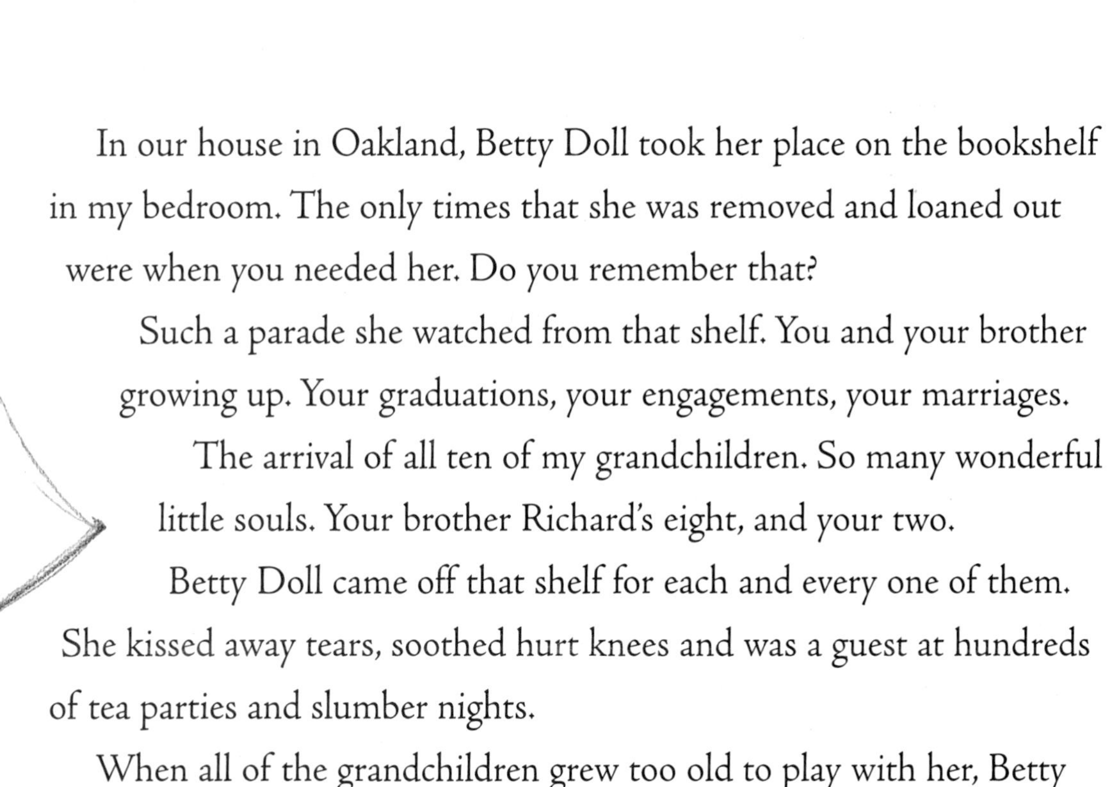

You don't know this, but the day I found out that I had cancer, I got Betty Doll off from that shelf and held her again. We cried together.

Just touching that now-faded dress reminded me of Aunt Mala and that glorious summer in Chicago. It reminded me of Momma and Dad, their farm, Michigan Augusts, the day she got lost in the snowstorm and was found again. She brought back the sound of katydids, nuthatches, meadowlarks. She helped me remember swims in that old pond near the edge of our woods.

It made me feel better.

And now, my darlin', I know you need Betty Doll. I had put her away because she had become as fragile as I now am. Hold her close to your heart.

She'll help you remember such warm things.

But most of all, when you look into her face, I want you to remember how much I love you.

I will always love you . . . and that, my darlin', will NEVER end.

Love,

Mom

° ° °

Mary Ellen Barber won her battle against cancer and lived out her years with style, humor and endless loyalty to her children.

On May 13, 1996, she passed into eternity. One of her great-granddaughters asked, "Where did Gramma go?"

We answered, "On a long journey ahead of us."

o o o

To the loving memory of my mother,
Mary Ellen Gaw Barber (1913–1996)

PATRICIA LEE GAUCH, EDITOR

PUFFIN BOOKS
Published by Penguin Group
Penguin Young Readers Group,
345 Hudson Street, New York, New York 10014, U.S.A.
Penguin Books Ltd, 80 Strand, London WC2R ORL, England
Penguin Books Australia Ltd, 250 Camberwell Road, Camberwell, Victoria 3124, Australia
Penguin Books Canada Ltd, 10 Alcorn Avenue, Toronto, Ontario, Canada M4V 3B2
Penguin Books (N.Z.) Ltd, 182-190 Wairau Road, Auckland 10, New Zealand

First published in the United States of America by Philomel Books,
a division of Penguin Putnam Books for Young Readers, 2001
Published by Puffin Books, a division of Penguin Young Readers Group, 2004

3 5 7 9 10 8 6 4 2

Designed by Semadar Megged
Text set in 16-point Adobe Jenson.

THE LIBRARY OF CONGRESS HAS CATALOGED THE PHILOMEL EDTION AS FOLLOWS:
Polacco, Patricia.
Betty Doll / Patricia Polacco.
p. cm.
ISBN: 0-399-23638-4 (hc)
1. Barber, Mary Ellen, d. 1996—Juvenile literature. 2. Union City Region (Mich.)—Biography—Juvenile literature. [1. Polacco, Patricia—Family. 2. Barber, Mary Ellen, d. 1996. 3. Dolls. 4. Mothers and daughters. 5. Women—Biography.]
I. Title.
CT275.B3674 P65 2001 977.4'21—dc21 [B] 00-040650

Puffin Books ISBN 0-14-240196-X

Printed in the United States of America